Tunnel of Terror
and Other Spooky Stories

J.B. Stamper

SCHOLASTIC INC.
New York Toronto London Auckland Sydney
Mexico City New Delhi Hong Kong

Cover illustration by
Tim Jessell

Interior illustrations by
Norm Lanting

"Tunnel of Terror" from TALES FOR THE MIDNIGHT HOUR: STORIES OF HORROR by J.B. Stamper. Copyright © 1977 by J.B. Stamper. Published by Scholastic Inc. Reprinted by permission.

"The Magic Vanishing Box" and "The Snipe Hunt" from STILL MORE TALES FROM THE MIDNIGHT HOUR: 13 STORIES OF HORROR by J.B. Stamper. Copyright © 1989 by J.B. Stamper. Published by Scholastic Inc. Reprinted by permission.

"The Shortcut" from MORE TALES FROM THE MIDNIGHT HOUR: 13 STORIES OF HORROR by J.B. Stamper. Copyright © 1987 by J.B. Stamper. Published by Scholastic Inc. Reprinted by permission.

ISBN 0-439-31288-4

SCHOLASTIC, READ 180, and associated logos and designs are trademarks and/or registered trademarks of Scholastic Inc. LEXILE is a trademark of MetaMetrics, Inc.

4   5   6   7   8   9   10   23   10 09 08 07

Contents

1 Tunnel of Terror

In the late summer, just before school started, Ellen always went to the Ohio State Fair with her friends. This year she set off for the state capital early one hot, summer morning with her friends, Jane and Diane. They laughed and talked all the way to Columbus on the two-hour trip. Arriving at the fair, they joined the crowd of people circling the dusty midway lined with food stands, rides, and other amusements.

By late afternoon, the three of them were tired and a little bored. They had seen nothing new from last year. Still, they decided to walk around the midway just one more time.

They passed the ice cream and hot dog and waffle stands. They looked over the Ferris wheel, the Wild Mouse and all the other rides again. And they walked by the freak show advertisements showing the fat lady, the Siamese twins, and the man with a rubber mouth.

Then they passed a small passageway they hadn't noticed before. Ellen suggested they follow it to see what was at the end. The passage twisted around behind the canvas tents until it ended at a huge sign advertising something called The Tunnel of Terror. The sign showed a small boat traveling along a dark canal. Along one side of the canal was a scene with wax figures showing someone being guillotined in the French Revolution.

"Creepy," Jane said. "I wouldn't go in there."

Ellen wasn't sure what put the idea into her head, but suddenly she wanted to ride through the Tunnel of Terror. Maybe it was that the tunnel looked cool and she was weary of the searing heat of the midway. Or maybe it was that she was looking for something new in her life, some new experience that would be strange and different.

"Anybody dare me to go in?" she asked.

"Are you crazy?" Diane said.

"I dare you," Jane said.

"All right, I'll go," Ellen announced bravely. "I suppose you two are afraid."

"We'll pay your way, right, Diane?" Jane said. "But wild horses couldn't drag me in there."

The three walked up to the ticket booth. A grizzled old man sat in it, cleaning his fingernails with a penknife.

"One, please," Ellen said.

"You're going in alone, are you?" the old man asked, staring at her through his bushy eyebrows.

"I'm not afraid," Ellen said. "Where do I catch the boat?"

The old man motioned her behind the ticket booth. As she went around, Diane and Jane started to follow.

"No," the old man said, "you can't go any further. You didn't buy tickets."

Ellen tried to sound cheerful as she yelled good-bye to her friends. But the boat was old and creaking, and she shivered as she slipped into the moldy, leather seat.

The old man pulled a wooden handle beside the canal that started a gear in motion. Ellen was startled by the noise and turned around to look at him. His mouth was set in a wide grin that showed his dirty, decaying teeth. Then, suddenly, she saw nothing; the boat had glided into pitch-black darkness.

In the dark, Ellen noticed that her sense of hearing became very keen. There was the creaking drag of the boat along the canal. There was the slobbering lap of the water against the sides of the boat. Then there was a shriek that made her heart jump to her throat.

A second after the shriek, a spotlight flashed on. Two feet in front of the boat was a man stretched out on a torture rack, his arms tearing from their sockets. Ellen could see the red blood oozing from his skin. She closed her eyes and buried her face in her hands. How much longer would this last?

The boat jerked around a sharp turn. Then the shriek Ellen heard was her own. A slimy mass had just passed over her face. She crouched down in the boat, feeling sick to her stomach. If she could stay like this until the trip was over, maybe she could stand it. Why did she ever want to come in here, she asked herself. She would give anything to be out in the bright sunlight with her friends.

There was a rumbling sound in front of her. Then Ellen heard the sharp hit of metal against wood. She peeked from between her hands. It was the guillotine scene. A bloody head rolled from the victim's body into a bucket next to the guillotine's sharp blade.

She braced herself for the next scene as the boat took another sickening, sharp turn. She felt something wet, something furry, slip around her shoulders. She tried to contain her screams. It would go away, she told herself, just like the slimy mass before. But the wet fur seemed to press closer to her. She felt a weight get into the boat beside her. She screamed and screamed and screamed....

Outside, Jane and Diane were laughing about the noises coming from inside the Tunnel of Terror. They could see that the old man was enjoying it, too. He leered at them, with a strange grin on his face.

But then, the noise from the Tunnel of Terror seemed to change. The screaming became constant, taking on a shrill tone of madness. The two girls looked at each other uneasily. Jane walked up to the old man's ticket booth.

"Will she be coming out soon?" she asked him.

"In another few minutes," he answered, still grinning. "Getting her money's worth, isn't she?"

Jane walked back to where Diane stood at the end of the canal. "I don't like it. I wish she would come out."

Just then the air was split with a cry of terror so awful the two girls shuddered at the sound of it.

"Get her out of there!" Jane said, running up to the old man.

"Nothing I can do," he said.

The screaming went on in the tunnel. It was hysterical now. Then a louder sound pierced the air. An announcement was being made over the intercom of the fair grounds.

"Ladies and gentlemen. It is important that you stay calm and don't panic. A gorilla has escaped from the zoo. Please find a safe place to wait until it has been recaptured. Don't go anywhere alone. Let me repeat again, don't panic."

But the announcement came too late for Ellen. Her friends watched as she glided out of the tunnel, the gorilla sitting on the seat beside her.

They got Ellen out of the boat. And, miraculously, she was unharmed. Except for her mind, that is.

They had to take her to the state hospital in Pleasant Valley immediately.

Why had Ellen gone on that scary ride?

2 The Magic Vanishing Box

Ben had wandered into a part of the city that he'd never seen before. The streets were lined with antique shops and second-hand stores. As he passed by one old shop, Ben stopped to look at a display in its window. Sitting in the midst of the other antiques was a tattered, black top hat with an old stuffed rabbit popping out of it.

Ben wondered if it was a real magician's hat. Magic was his hobby. It was almost an obsession with him, in fact. He read everything he could about it and practiced tricks in his spare time.

Ben went to the shop door and read the sign: Curiosities of the Past. He pushed open the door and went inside. One glance around the small one-room shop told him it lived up to its name.

There were stuffed monkeys sitting beside huge brass candlesticks. There were life-size china dogs sitting on carved wooden boxes that looked like coffins. The shop was very curious, indeed.

Ben began to look through the knicknacks and larger items displayed on the tables and shelves in the room.

"May I help you?"

Ben whirled around at the sound of the voice. He saw a stooped old man looking at him with piercing eyes.

"I...I was just looking around," Ben stammered.

"Take your time, take your time," the man said. "I'll be in the back if you need me. Ring this bell if you want to buy anything." The man gestured to an old brass bell by the cash register and then hobbled off into the back of the store.

Ben shrugged his shoulders and continued to walk around the store. He took a closer look at the silk hat in the window. It was a magician's hat, but he had no need for another one. Ben wondered if there might be other magic tricks in the store, old ones that he'd never seen before.

For half an hour Ben lost track of the time as he searched through the jumble of odds and ends on display. Then something caught his eye. It was a shiny, black wood box about two feet square. Ben ran his hand over the smooth wood, the brass hinge at the front, and the brass-covered corners.

But what interested him most was the little brass plate on top of the box. It was engraved with the words: The Magic Vanishing Box. With care, Ben unlatched the brass hinge at the front of the box and lifted the lid. Inside, there was nothing, just the empty interior of the black wood. Then Ben caught sight of another brass plate on the inside of the lid. It too, was engraved with words:

DON'T CATCH YOUR HAND INSIDE THIS LID,
OR ELSE YOU'LL BE SORRY THAT YOU DID.

Ben carefully shut the lid on the box and stared at it for a long time. What was a magic vanishing box? It was probably some sort of joke. Still, Ben wanted it more than he'd wanted anything for a long time. He reached in his pocket to check the money he'd brought along for his trip into the city. Fifteen dollars. And he needed two dollars of that to get home. All he could spend on the box was thirteen dollars.

Ben picked up the box and carried it over to the counter by the cash register. He pressed his hand down on the bell. A shrill ding echoed through the store. Soon the old man came out from the back room. He looked at Ben; then he looked at the box. Slowly, a strange smile spread over his face.

An hour later, Ben was in his bedroom unwrapping the newspaper that the old man had bundled around the box. His hands were trembling as he set the shiny box on top of his desk. Again he read the words on the brass plate: The Magic Vanishing Box. Ben decided he couldn't wait any longer. He had to find out if he had spent his thirteen dollars foolishly. Carefully he opened the lid to the box and looked inside. There were no instructions except for the warning he'd read before:

DON'T CATCH YOUR HAND INSIDE THIS LID,
OR ELSE YOU'LL BE SORRY THAT YOU DID.

Ben gingerly opened the lid all the way and then looked around the room. What could he experiment with first? His eyes fell on the blue dictionary that sat on his desk. It would just fit into the box, and he wouldn't care in the least if it vanished.

Ben picked up the heavy book and set it into the bottom of the box. Then he cautiously closed the lid by holding onto its front brass hinge. He felt silly about taking the warning inside the box seriously. After all, it was probably just a practical joke. He snapped down the hinge into place and stood staring at the box. There were no magic words to say; no magic wand to wave. Ben waited for a few minutes, then he opened the lid.

The inside of the box was empty.

Ben stared at the empty, black space for a moment, then he picked up the box to look under it. Nothing was there. Carefully, he shut the lid and turned the box over and over, looking for the secret to its magic. He knew there must be a trick. Things didn't just vanish.

At last he found what he was looking for. On one side of the box, right beside the brass corner

decoration, was a small brass latch. Ben pulled it until it sprung; then a tiny drawer shot open from the side of the box.

Ben stared down at the weird things inside the drawer. There was a tiny blue book lying beside a small, life-like figure of a boy. Ben picked up the book first. He squinted to read the small print of the title. It was a dictionary, a perfect miniature version of his dictionary. He flipped through the pages, and then suddenly let it drop as though it had burned him. How had the box done that? What kind of magic did it have?

Ben's eyes were drawn to the small figure of the boy. It was only about two inches high and was dressed in old-fashioned clothes. The details of its face and clothing were so realistic that it could have been alive, except that it was so small.

Ben set the tiny book and the figure on his bookshelf. Then he shut the secret drawer, opened the box lid, and looked around his room for something else to test. He still couldn't believe this was happening to him.

He caught sight of his face in the mirror above his dresser. The freckles on his face were standing out against his white skin. He pinched his arm under his red football jersey, just to make sure he was awake. The box was the strangest trick he had ever used. And there was something even more strange. It didn't seem to be just a trick — it was real magic.

Ben picked up a pencil, put it in the box, and

shut the lid. A minute later, he pushed the latch on the secret drawer. It shot open, and inside was a perfect replica of the pencil, so little that Ben could hardly pick it up.

Ben looked at the clock in his room. He knew his parents would be home soon, and he wanted to keep the box a secret. But he had to try the trick just one more time. This time he would put in something unusual. He looked up and saw his transistor radio. Would the radio still be able to play music if it were turned into a miniature?

Ben opened the lid of the box and reached up for his radio. It just fit inside the box. As he started to close the lid, Ben saw that the radio's antenna was sticking up. He reached one hand inside the box to push the antenna down.

Just then his mother's voice called from downstairs, "Ben, we're home."

Ben swung his head around in panic. Then the heavy, black lid of the box slammed down on his hand. For a second it hurt. Then Ben felt nothing.

For a year the police searched for Ben. But the only clues they had to work with were the strange black box and the tiny book and figure they found in his room. Finally the police gave up. Ben's parents cleaned out his room and gave away his belongings. And eventually the black box made its way back to the old antique shop where Ben had bought it.

The old man sat it back on its shelf. It waited there for another boy to come in and buy it. And that boy would find its secret drawer—and, inside the drawer, a small life-like figure of a boy with freckles wearing a red football jersey.

Why couldn't the police find Ben? What happened to him?

3 The Shortcut

People ask me why I've changed. They say I'm too quiet, too withdrawn; some even say I've become a little strange. Well, it's true, I have changed. Ever since that night last summer....

It had been a perfect summer day. I had gone swimming in a pond a few miles from my uncle's farm where I was staying for the month of July. A group of kids who lived in the nearby town were there, too. After swimming, we bought some food and had a picnic in the park. Before I realized how late it was, the sky had started to grow dim, with the twilight. The rest of the kids started for home in the town. I was the only one who had to ride the long way to my uncle's house. I raced my bike hard up the big hill outside town in the direction of the farm. By the time I got to the crest, I had to stop. I was so exhausted that my legs trembled. I stood still on the top of the hill, alone on the road, with my bike leaning against me. I was too tired to go on, too tired to do anything but watch the setting sun. It had sunk so low that it looked like a huge, burning ball in the dark blue sky. Blood-red streaks shot out from it across the horizon.

I shuddered suddenly and felt a chill pass through my body. It seemed that I was the only person alive in the world. This part of the country was remote and lonely, and I wasn't familiar with it.

Looking down the hill, I saw where the road split into two forks. I had driven down this hill with my uncle several times. He had taken the road to the right, which was hilly and went past farmhouses. I knew it would be a long, hard ride to get home on that road. When I had asked my uncle about the road to the left, he had said it was the shortcut. Then he had mumbled something about people never taking it. I couldn't remember exactly what he had said.

All around me, the color of the sky deepened to a purplish black. The last red rays of the sunset had faded from the horizon. I knew I had to get back to my uncle's farm as fast as I could. I swung my leg over the bike and pushed off down the hill. When the road split ahead of me, I took the left turn… onto the shortcut.

My bike shot down the old dirt road, raising a cloud of dust around me. In the dim light I could see that there were no other tracks on the ground. I started to put on the brakes, suddenly wishing I had taken the more familiar road. Then I realized that I had been steadily coasting downhill. To turn back would mean climbing uphill again. I rode on, down the deserted road.

Finally the ground leveled out, and I had to push hard on the pedals to keep up my speed. My legs ached, but I ignored the pain. I was flying down the road in almost total darkness now. The only light came from a thin moon that hung like a sickle in the black sky.

Then even that light was blotted out by a cloud that moved across the moon. At first I couldn't sense where the road was in front of me. But slowly my eyes, like a cat's, grew used to seeing in the dark. I followed the road that stretched like a ghostly ribbon through the darkness on both sides.

Suddenly the front wheel of my bike hit a hard bump. I struggled to keep it under control, gripping the handlebars so tightly that my hands ached.

The clouds over the moon parted just then. Ahead of me, bathed in eerie moonlight, was an old graveyard. Standing in the middle of the white tombstones was the huge black shadow of a decaying house.

A lump of fear rose in my throat. I started to pump my legs on the pedals as fast as I could. I drew nearer and nearer to the cemetery. But my bike seemed to be going slower and slower. Then, through the panic in my mind, the truth came to me. The front tire of my bike was losing air. Its slow, hissing sound mocked me as I struggled uselessly to pedal forward on the road.

The bike slowed down to a crawl, then it came to a total stop right in front of the graveyard. I looked at the white tombstones, lined up like soldiers in the moonlight. They seemed to stare back at me with curious, sinister eyes hidden in their cold marble.

For a minute I thought about running away, leaving my bike behind. But I forced myself to stoop down and inspect the front wheel. As I had feared, all the air had leaked out.

I heard a noise behind me, a strange rattling noise coming from the cemetery. I jumped to my feet and cowered against the bike. Again I considered running. But then, all was deadly silent. I reached down and pulled the air pump from the crossbar of my bike.

My hands were shaking, and I dropped the pump against the metal spokes of the back wheel. The noise echoed from one tombstone to another as I bent to pick it up. Still trembling, I found the tire valve and fastened the pump onto it just in time, for then the moon disappeared behind the clouds again, and I was left in total darkness.

I started the pump, afraid to think what I would do if it didn't work. But it did work. The air went in and out, in and out, sounding like heavy breathing. I was breathing hard, too, my breath coming in short gasps. Then, suddenly, I stopped. The sound, the same rattling sound that I had heard before, came from behind me again. The pump hissed louder and louder as I worked it harder. But the rattling grew louder and louder, too. It was coming toward me, closer and closer, through the black night.

I had to escape whatever was making that horrible sound. I pulled the pump off the tire and threw it on the ground by the graveyard. Jumping up, I started to swing my leg over the bike. Then I felt something that made my blood run cold. Five sharp points were stroking the top of my head. They seemed to dig into my brain.

I tried to tell myself that it was the branch of a tree, but the five points began to move down toward my neck. My legs were numbed with fear, but I forced them onto the pedals. Then, with one great lunge of fear, I shot forward on the road.

Whatever had been reaching for my neck was gone now. I had escaped its horrid grip. The bike flew through the darkness, leaving the tombstones to stare at my fleeing back. My body felt as cold as death. Still, my legs worked automatically, pushing the pedals up and down, carrying me away from whatever had touched me in front of the cemetery.

I shot through the darkness, going as fast as I could until my front tire hit another bump. I kept control of the wheels, but a sickening fear spread through my mind. The sound, that horrid rattling sound, was still right behind me!

I pumped harder and harder on the pedals. My breath came in short, painful gasps. I rode on for several minutes, thinking I was safe. Then I heard it again, the rattling. I was afraid to turn around, afraid to see what was chasing me down the dark, lonely road. Time and time again, the rattling sounded behind me. It played on my nerves until I thought I would descend into madness and never return.

Finally, in the moonlight, I caught sight of my uncle's farm. I turned onto the road that led up to his house. My uncle was standing in front, gazing down the road, waiting for me. As soon as I saw him, I tried to tell myself that it had all been my imagination—the staring tombstones, the strange rattling. I rode my bike up to where he stood and jumped off, breathing so desperately that I couldn't speak. I waited for him to say something; but, instead, a look of horror came over his face. He was staring at the seat of my bike.

Trembling, I turned around. There, clamped onto the back of the seat in a grisly death grip, was the rattling, bony hand… of a skeleton.

What did you think the noise would turn out to be?

4 The Snipe Hunt

The twelve boys sat around the campfire, roasting marshmallows on sticks after finishing their evening meal. Their faces were lit by the jumping flames of the fire—eight older faces and four younger faces. The older boys looked relaxed and confident. But the younger boys looked tense and worried. Tonight they would be tested.

Ty, who was only eleven, was the youngest boy in the group. Jimmy, Paul, and Brad were twelve, but this was their initiation night, too. If they made it through tonight, they'd be let into the camping club.

"What do you think they'll do to us?" Ty whispered to Brad, who sat beside him by the

fire. "I don't know," Brad answered. "Ask Paul. His brother is one of the older guys."

Ty turned to Paul on his other side. "What will they do to us tonight?" he asked in a low voice.

"I heard my brother talk about a snipe hunt," Paul whispered back.

"A snipe hunt?" Ty said. "What's that?"

Before Paul could answer, Mark, one of the leaders, started to talk. Everyone paid attention.

"I want to warn you younger guys about something," Paul began. "These woods are pretty far from civilization. We're out here in the middle of nowhere by ourselves, and we have to be careful. Nobody knows for sure what kind of animals are in the woods— wolves, bears, bobcats. We've had our supper… but they might still be hungry."

Ty looked at Brad nervously. Brad's face had grown serious, too.

"And there's another thing I have to tell you," Mark went on. "I heard something on the radio today, just before we left to come here. I've been trying to decide whether or not to tell you, but now I think I should. A murderer escaped from the state penitentiary in Columbus last night. The police haven't caught him yet, but they know he headed in a northwest direction. They figure he's covering about twenty miles a day… and, well, you know about where that would take him."

"This place is about twenty miles northwest of Columbus," Brad said.

"Yeah, that's right," Mark said. "But now that we're here, I don't think we should call off our camping trip just because of an escaped murderer."

Ty noticed that his hands were shaking so much that his marshmallow stick was moving up and down. The marshmallow had burned to a crisp.

"So, be careful, and report anything strange that you hear or see in the woods," Mark said.

Just then, there was a loud crack in the woods behind the younger boys. They all jumped and turned around.

"What was that?" Ty whimpered.

The older boys laughed.

"What's the matter, Ty, getting a little scared?" Robbie asked.

"It's too early to get scared," Mark said. "You four guys have to go on your snipe hunt yet. Go to your tents and get a flashlight and get back here in five minutes."

The boys got up from the campfire and walked back to their tents through the chilly night air. The moon was full enough to light their way, but the dark shadows of the trees made it hard to see far into the dense woods. They all got their flashlights from their packs and started back to the campfire.

"Was he telling the truth about the murderer?" Ty whispered to Paul on the way back.

"I don't know," Paul said. "And I don't want to find out."

"I wish this were over with!" Jimmy said.

Mark was waiting for them. He was standing by the fire with four burlap bags.

"These are the bags you use to catch the snipe," he said, handing one to each of the boys.

"How do we know it's a snipe?" Jimmy asked. "What's it look like?"

"Listen, you'll know when you see it," Mark said. "Now be quiet and listen to the rules."

The four boys clutched their bags in one hand and their flashlights in the other and listened.

"Each of you has to walk in a different direction from the campfire," Mark began. "Count how many steps you're taking, and when you get to two hundred fifty, stop. That'll take you far enough away from the light of the campfire. Snipes are too smart to come near a fire."

"What about our flashlights?" Ty asked. "Won't they scare away the snipes?" Some of the older boys started to laugh. But Mark cut them off.

"Use your flashlights while you're walking out the two hundred fifty steps. Then turn them off and wait."

"How long do we wait?" Brad asked.

"Till we call you in with this whistle," Mark said. He sounded three short whistles and then three long whistles.

"Any questions?"

The four boys looked at each other uneasily.

"What about those other animals you talked about?" Paul said. "What if we see them?"

"Or the murderer?" Ty added with a whisper.

Mark just shrugged his shoulders and looked at his watch.

"Time to start walking," he said. "And remember to count two hundred fifty steps. Then turn off your lights."

Ty glanced over at Paul and Brad and Jimmy. They looked as scared as he felt. Mark told Brad to start walking toward the north. Then he sent Jimmy off to the east and Paul to the west.

"Ty," he said, "you walk south."

Ty gulped, switched on his flashlight, and turned to face the south. He took a step away from the campfire and started counting. At first he took normal steps; then he took shorter ones that wouldn't carry him so far into the woods.

Ty had counted a hundred steps when he

first turned around. The campfire was just a yellowish glow in the darkness of the woods. He shone his light into the woods in front of him and started walking and counting again. The dead leaves that had fallen from the trees crackled under his feet. Several times a raised root caught at his foot and almost sent him sprawling onto the ground. Night animals scurried away as his light pierced the darkness. Once an owl swooped down across the moon and passed its shadow over him.

Ty had counted two hundred steps. He turned around. The thick trees blocked out the campfire now. He couldn't hear the older boys' voices and laughter anymore. He hoped he would be able to hear Mark's whistles.

Fifty more steps to go. Ty forced his legs to go on through the woods until he had counted to two hundred fifty. Then he swung his flashlight around in the place where he had stopped. It was a small clearing that had a thick carpet of leaves covering the ground.

The flashlight picked up the outline of a big tree stump about three yards from where Ty stood. Tall hickory trees with shaggy bark stood around the small clearing. Ty pointed the light up and saw their long limbs reaching up to the sky like the arms of skeletons. Then he flicked off the flashlight and crouched down on the ground. He clutched the burlap bag in both hands and waited. The snipe hunt had begun.

The wind blew through the tree branches above him, making a strange rattling sound. Ty waited and waited. Once he saw a big shadow move near the tree stump. He froze, not sure if it was a bear or a man. But the shadow disappeared and didn't come back again. Ty's hands were growing numb with cold and fatigue. He thought he would go crazy if he had to stay out in the dark alone one more minute.

Then he heard a strange noise come from the direction of the tree stump. It was a shrill animal sound, unlike anything he'd ever heard before. He strained his eyes to see in the moonlight. He glimpsed the pale, gray body of an animal walking toward him from the tree stump. It kept making its shrill call as it slowly wobbled across the bed of leaves.

Ty had never seen an animal like it before. He knew it must be a snipe. He leaned over and set the burlap bag down in front of where the animal was walking. It didn't seem to be able to see the bag and headed straight toward it. Ty held his breath until the small animal had walked into his bag. Then he shut the opening of the bag and gripped it tight.

A minute later, three short whistles and three long whistles cut through the stillness of the night. Ty picked up his flashlight and started to run in the direction of the sound. He held the sack away from his body and listened as the animal began to make shrill noises in a panic.

Ty burst into the light of the campfire with his breath coming in short gasps. Everyone else was standing there, waiting for him. Paul, Brad, and Jimmy had already made it back.

"We thought the murderer might have got you, Ty," Mark said. The boys around the campfire laughed. Ty stood by the fire with his bag, waiting for Mark to ask about the snipe. But Mark didn't even look at his bag.

"The four of you did a great job," he said, looking at Paul, Brad, Jimmy, and Ty. "None of you chickened out. You all passed the test, and now you're in the club."

"But what about the snipe?" Ty asked.

"Come on, Ty, that was just a joke," Robbie said.

"Ty, what do you have in that bag?" Mark asked.

"A snipe," Ty answered.

Just then, the animal cried its weird call.

"He caught something!" Brad said. "Let's see it."

Everyone jumped up and crowded around Ty.

"Drop the bag into this box, Ty," Mark ordered, pulling over an empty food box.

Carefully Ty put the bag into the box and let go of its opening. The other boys peered down into the box. Slowly, the animal Ty had caught crawled out of the bag. It turned its face up at the boys staring down at it. Then it let out a hiss and a shrill screech.

The boys all jumped back.

"What is it?" Robbie asked.

"That's the strangest-looking animal I've ever seen," Mark said.

Again the boys stared down at the animal. It had a thick, stout body. Its paws had sharp white claws and its long tail ended in a jagged point. But its head was weirdest of all. The ears were high and pointed, and the mouth had long, sharp teeth.

"I think it's a baby that was just born," Mark said. "Its eyes are still shut!"

"Look, it's trying to open them," Ty said.

Suddenly the animal's strange eyes flew open. They were orange and glowed in the night.

"Is it a snipe?" Ty asked.

"I don't know," Mark said. "Nobody's ever seen a snipe. We just made up the snipe hunt to scare you guys."

"So what is it?" Brad asked.

The animal started to shriek louder and louder and show its pointed teeth at the boys. One by one, they backed uneasily away from the box.

"What was that?" Robbie suddenly asked, turning around to look into the woods. "I thought I heard something out there." "Me, too," said Paul.

The boys fell silent and listened as the animal in the box made its shrill call over and over again. And from different parts of the woods, the same call came back.

"What are we going to do?" Ty asked.

"I don't know," Mark answered, looking scared.

The calls from the woods became louder and louder. Then the leaves on the floor of the woods started to rustle. The boys huddled closer together around the campfire.

Suddenly Ty screamed and pointed to the woods. A pair of strange orange eyes were glowing from the shadows of the trees. They were like the eyes of the animal in the box, only bigger. Then Brad screamed and pointed to the opposite side of the campfire. The boys whirled around and saw another pair of orange eyes glowing in the woods. Then they saw another and another and another.

The animal in the box made a weird noise from deep in its throat. Then from the woods, like a nightmarish echo, came the same noise from all around the boys.

Mark looked at Ty's face, which had turned white with fear.

"You caught a snipe, all right," he said.

Then they turned to look at the orange eyes in the woods. The eyes had started to glow brighter. And they were moving in closer and closer... toward the twelve boys huddled together around the campfire.

Why was everyone surprised that Ty caught a snipe?

Meet the Author

I have written several books of scary stories—all of them with twist endings. That's my specialty. I loved to read while growing up, especially mysteries and stories full of suspense. I practiced being scary by experimenting on my little brother.

Many of my stories are based on places I have visited or stories I have read or heard. For example, "The Shortcut" is set on the lonely country lane leading to my grandparents' house. "The Snipe Hunt" is based on an old Boy Scout story my brother told me.

I love getting letters from my readers. Most of them begin, "Dear Mr. Stamper . . ." (But "Dear Ms. Stamper . . ." would be much nicer.) My fans always ask where I get my ideas from. I get them from reading lots of stories myself and, of course, from my own weird imagination!

—*J.B. Stamper*